I Help Around The House:

A Picture Book About Being Responsible & Making Chores Fun

By
Paige Moss

Other Books by Paige Moss

I Help Around The House: Picture Book About Being Responsible & Making Chores Fun

I am Happy & Thankful Because...: Expressing Gratitude at Home (Picture Book)

More Books by Paige Moss

amazon.com/author/paigemoss

Dedication

To my daughters and granddaughters who have truly inspired me.

I love you

Paige Moss

Hi.
My name is Abby.

I live at home with my mom and sister.

I have my own room.
I am responsible for keeping it clean.

I have lots of toys.

I love playing with my toys every day.

I think I like my stuffed animals the most.

I keep my room clean most of the time.

I help around the house, too.
Sometimes I don't feel like
cleaning my room.

If I don't, it gets messier and messier.
Mom doesn't like it at all.

When I do finally clean my room, it's a lot more work.

If I pick up my things every day then, it's not so bad.

My friends are good at helping around the house, too.

My friend, Amy, helps with washing dishes.

My friends, Adam and Stacy,

help take out the trash.

Kirk helps his father wash the car every week.

Sarah helps her mom clean the family room.

Sometimes when mom asks for help around the house, we play music and sing.

I pretend I am singing in a band.

My dog Daisy is so cute.

My sister and I take turns giving Daisy a bath.

I try and find ways to make my chores fun.

I sing. I dance. I use my imagination all the time.

I really like to play pretend.

Sometimes when I'm putting my stuffed animals away,

I pretend they are in a parade.

You can help your parents
and feel really good about it.

Helping around the house is not always fun, but...

our parents really like it when we help.

Helping around the house can be fun, just use your imagination.

Dear reader:

I hope you enjoyed reading this book. There are a series of books created to assist children in their daily lives. These books were created to help children stay motivated, have fun and, most of all, remain balanced in this world of ups and downs.

To read more books from me, please visit:
amazon.com/author/paigemoss.

Also, please write a review for this book. It is greatly appreciated.

Made in the USA
Middletown, DE
23 October 2021